THE CARR HOUSE CATS GO EXPLORING

Dedicated to our beloved Cats: Misty and Whiskers.

by Darien Ross

Illustrations by Michelle Coburn

Order this book online at www.trafford.com
or email orders@trafford.com

Most Trafford titles are also available at major online book retailers.

Illustrations by Michelle Coburn

Printed in the United States of America.

ISBN: 978-1-4907-3855-0 (sc)
        978-1-4907-3854-3 (e)

Our mission is to efficiently provide the world's finest, most comprehensive book publishing service, enabling every author to experience success. To find out how to publish your book, your way, and have it available worldwide, visit us online at www.trafford.com

Trafford rev. 07/25/2014

www.trafford.com
North America & international
toll-free: 1 888 232 4444 (USA & Canada)
fax: 812 355 4082

THE CARR HOUSE CATS GO EXPLORING

Darien Ross

Illustrations by Michelle Coburn

Emily Carr House sat quietly on Government Street watching people walk by.

Also watching from one of the windows was Misty one of the Carr House Cats. He was new to the house, he had only been living under its old roof for a few months but by now he knew every room and every creak of the floor boards by heart. He knew where to hide, where to pounce and where to peek through the curtains to watch the outside world.

Misty had never been outside. He was only a tiny kitten when he had first been brought to Carr House, but now he was on the verge of becoming a CAT, and CATS went outside. Just as he was thinking this over Whiskers, Misty's brother, came into the room. Whiskers had a worried look upon his face.

"Today is the day we go outside," he said, looking scared. Misty nodded his head. He was the older of the two and always looked out for his little brother.

"It will not be too bad, I heard our Humans talking, they said they would leave the door open so that we can come and go. We won't be locked outside."

Whiskers smiled, "I wonder what's out there? I wonder what this house looks like from the outside? I know this place so well, I would never have dreamed that there was more to learn."

Misty agreed. They had been told by their Humans that they lived in a special house and that not all cats were as lucky as them. For they lived in Emily Carr House, the birthplace of one of Canada's greatest painters, Emily Carr.

She was born upstairs in the very room where Whiskers was so fond of taking naps. She had grown up in the very rooms they now loved to explore. As he sat there, Misty began to wonder if a young Emily had found the same hiding spots as he?

Just about then they heard one of their Humans go to the front door and open it. The cool air whistled in and clung to their fur and straightened their whiskers. They each took a deep breath, and walked out the door.

The world was different outdoors, the ground was cold on their paws, noises were louder coming from every direction but they loved it! Skipping down the front steps, they suddenly stopped part way and stared at everything.

The home they have been living in, is a great Big yellow house with a turn about driveway and a lush garden.

The Carr House Cats knew they lived in a city called Victoria and that their home was also a museum. This old Victorian home was open to visitors from all around the world so that they might walk into the rooms where a great artist grew up learning to draw.

Now though had come the time in their young lives when the Carr House Cats would discover the surrounding grounds. Misty led the way, his nose in the air sniffing at all new smells. They came around the side of the house and saw bushes lining the fence and flowers in the garden.

"It's so different out here," Whiskers said with a grin, trotting up to Misty. "I wonder what.. the garden holds?"

Misty, who sometimes liked to pull pranks on his brother turned to him and said in a deep voice, "Do you really want to know what the garden holds?" Whiskers stopped, and nodded his head. Misty puffed up his chest and stretched out his paws "They say this garden has a monster, a HUGE creature, with a thousand eyes and sharp claws." Whiskers' yellow eyes grew big and his fur began to shake as Misty continued " Be careful. When you turn your back that's when it decides to STRIKE!"

Just then something popped out of the bushes! Misty and Whiskers both jumped! They stared at the creature as it dusted itself off. Whiskers shook his head, now no longer afraid of this creature. His brother had played a trick on him. He looked closer at the thing that had sprung from the bushes. It was a large bird.

"Who are you?" Misty asked.

"Who am I?" asked the strange thing, offended. "Do you not know who I am?" Both cats shook their heads.

"I'm Percy Peacock, and I have lived in these parts for many years - just over yonder at Beacon Hill Park. Whom am I addressing?"

"I'm Whiskers, and this is my brother Misty, we live here and have done so for just a few months. This is our first day out of the yellow house."

Percy smiled, "You live in The Emily Carr House? Oh, how lucky you two are, Emily Carr is my inspiration. I happen to be an artist myself. I often come here to be inspired. You are so lucky to be living in her home. You say though this is your first time out of the house?"

"Yes, we were too young before to be let out, but now we are of age. So today was the day we were allowed outdoors. We had only just started exploring when we saw you," Misty said. He too was no longer afraid of this colourful neighbour.

"What kind of artist are you? Are you a painter?" Whiskers asked.

"Oh, yes. I paint almost every day. It's my passion," said Percy Peacock puffing up his feathers. " I have often painted scenes from this lovely garden. Since this is your first day of exploring allow me to give you the grand tour."

Misty and Whiskers liked that idea very much. Percy Peacock started by guiding them around the house, pointing out special details – like the fancy finials along the roofline. Through a little break in the trees he showed them another yellow house. This small little bungalow had belonged to Alice Carr, Emily's favourite sister.

As it happened a very handsome orange cat now lived there. His name was Norris and when he saw the Carr House Cats in the garden he ambled over to say 'how do you do'? He was a friendly cat, a few years old, but still a kitten at heart.

Soon other friendly neighbours joined them in the garden. Percy Peacock pointed up into a nearby tree and introduced the cats to Rochester the Raccoon.

"Glad to have you in the neighbourhood fellas. Hope you two are tree climbers- always love the company."

Percy Peacock then introduced the Cats to the lovely bunny, Lady Pepper and Suze, the elder cat, who were out tending to the flowers. Lady Pepper promised that she would hold a garden party in their honour.

"Everyone has been so kind," purred Misty.

"I quite agree. Oh, I do hope our Humans will let us out again soon. Norris has promised to teach me some new tricks and imagine a garden party with lovely fresh cream! I can't wait," trilled Whiskers.

"Yes, we are all very lucky to live in a neighbourhood such as this one," said Percy Peacock.

Just then the cats heard their names being called. They had been out quite long enough and it now was dinner time.

"Thank you for showing us around Percy and introducing us to all our new friends," said Whiskers.

"My pleasure Carr House Cats, I will see you next time you adventure out of doors."

Misty and Whiskers said their goodbyes and hurried back into the house where dinner was waiting for them.

As they ate they thought about all the things they'd seen and the creatures they had met. The Carr House Cats were no longer afraid of the outdoors and could hardly wait till tomorrow.

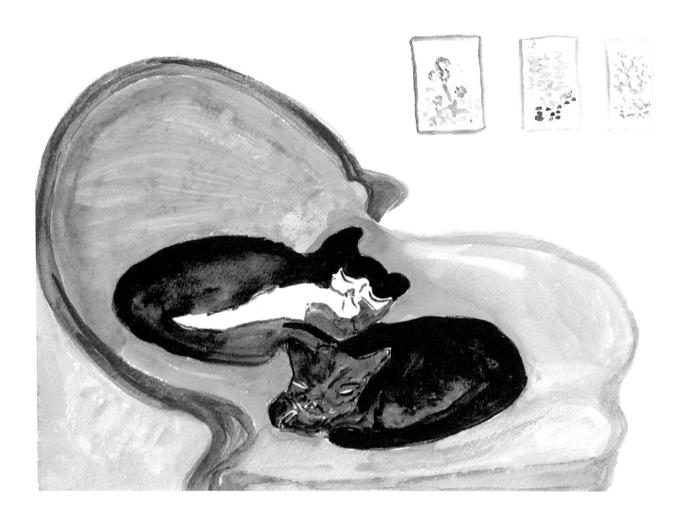

But all the day's adventures had made them very drowsy and so they curled up side by side and contentedly fell asleep.

Emily Carr House Neighbours

Meet the characters in the Carr House Cats books, who are all based on real critters that have lived in the house or in the neighbourhood over the years.

Percy Peacock

Peacocks are a common sight in the side garden of Emily Carr House; their home being only just a short distance away in Beacon Hill Park. Percy has been known to take a stroll down the street and come into our gates for a quick look around before heading back up to the Park.

Rochester the Raccoon

Rochester lives in the nearby trees surrounding the house; sometimes if you are lucky you will catch him on a day time stroll along the fence. He enjoys checking out the neighbourhood before climbing back into the trees for an afternoon nap.

Suze

Suze lived next door in the pink house on the corner, an older cat that would keep to her garden, but she had made good friends with Misty and Whiskers. She enjoyed smelling the flowers and simple pleasantries of the day.

Norris

Norris was the first cat to grace Emily Carr House with feline paws after many years of it being without inhabitants. He lived behind the fence at the home of Emily's sister, Alice . Norris would come for visits on rainy days for a saucer of milk and to play dress up with the girls that live here at the house. A very well natured cat that always had a glint of mischief in his eye.

Lady Pepper

Pepper was a rabbit that lived on the grounds of Emily Carr House before Misty and Whiskers had arrived. When the kittens were introduced to her, she became something of a mother to them. They would spend their time grooming each other behind the ears, then all curling down for a nap. A truly special rabbit.

Misty

Misty is our official greeter, often you may find him lounging on the front counter. He loves to be admired and spoken to by the many folk who visit us. At times aloof, Misty can be coaxed to have his photo taken when it suits his fancy.

Whiskers

A little shy but very sweet natured, Whiskers, prefers to be a behind the scenes kind of fellow. He'll peek out from beneath tables and chairs to watch the world go by. Despite his reserve, Whiskers has been known to have a friendly chat with guests.

About the Author

Like Emily and her sisters, Darien Ross and her sister have grown up in Emily Carr House. Darien is inspired by Emily's art, writings and her deep love of animals. This is Darien's second Carr House Cats book and she can't wait to start on a third.

About the Illustrator

Michelle Coburn loves to draw. It led to studying fine arts and a teaching career. Marianne is her seven-year-old granddaughter who joined in this project as they visited together in France, where Marianne Emily Goetzke Coburn lives. Together they read through the story- drawing and discussing how it would look. Michelle is, also, the aunt of the author.

About Emily Carr and her House

Emily Carr (1871-1945) is renowned as an artist, writer and lover of nature. She was born at 207 Government Street, Victoria, B.C., Canada. Her childhood home is now a National and Provincial Historic Site owned by the people of British Columbia. Emily Carr House is open to visitors from all over the world as an interpretive centre for this fascinating Canadian.

Edwards Brothers Malloy
Thorofare, NJ USA
September 16, 2014